"**H**ey!" I called, "Hey! Wait up!"

I dodged back into the barn and jumped down into the pile of hay below. I sneezed once, then made for the door to run after him. But I didn't need to; he was in the barn waiting for me.

All of a sudden I wasn't so eager to say hi. In fact, I was kind of scared of him. He was taller than me, but he was spindly, weak-looking. I wasn't afraid he was going to beat me up or anything. It was something else. Maybe it was the way he had crossed the door-yard and entered the barn in less time than it took me to jump out of the loft. Maybe it was the way he stared at me as if there was no brain behind his washed-out eyes.

Or maybe it was the smell.

I didn't realize it at the time, but now I think that strange odor was coming from him.

It was like the odor of earth, the unfamiliar scent of things that were once alive, like rotting squirrels and leaves, mixed with the smell of things that would never live, like water and stones.

༄ Also by Joseph A. Citro ༄

༄ Fiction ༄
*Shadow Child**
Guardian Angels
*Lake Monsters**
*The Gore**
*Deus-X: The Reality Conspiracy**
*Not Yet Dead**

༄ Books That Might Not Be Fiction ༄
Green Mountain Ghosts, Ghouls, and Unsolved Mysteries
Passing Strange—True Tales of New England Hauntings and Horrors
Green Mountains, Dark Tales
Cursed in New England: Stories of Damned Yankees
Curious New England: The Unconventional Traveler's Guide to Eccentric Destinations
Weird New England
The Vermont Ghost Guide
The Vermont Monster Guide
Joe Citro's Weird Vermont—Strange Tales of Vermont and Vermonters
Vermont's Haunts—Tall Tales and True from the Green Mountain State

(*indicates titles available from Crossroad Press)

Not Yet Dead

Joseph A. Citro

Crossroad Press

❧ CONTENTS ❧

❧ INTRODUCTION ❧

I don't write short stories. I guess I'm just too long-winded. My pathway to publication was the road not taken. I avoided conventional approaches such as spending time as a newspaper reporter or writing magazine articles before working my way "up" to short fiction.

Instead, perhaps ill-advisedly, I leapt directly into novels. In time, I switched my attention to book-length collections of local folklore and strange-but-(allegedly)-true phenomena.

So where did this handful of short stories come from?

I wrote them all by invitation. In the late 1980s my fiction was starting to see print as I tried to establish myself as a novelist. As my books appeared and were reviewed, accomplished writers would invite me to submit a new short story to a developing anthology.

J.N. Williamson, an award-winning editor and prolific writer of scary tales, was the first to do so. He asked me to write a story for his prestigious anthology series, *Masques*. And so "Them Bald-Headed Snays" appeared in 1989. I was pleased to find myself "between the covers" with such writers as Ray Bradbury, Dan Simmons, and Ed Gorman.

Subsequently, this first published short story was reprinted in *The Year's Best Fantasy and Horror*. After that, a few more invitations trickled in. Stanley Wiater asked for a contribution to his anthology, *After the Darkness*. So, in 1993, "Kirby" was born.

And so it went.

When I stopped writing novels, the invitations stopped.

In my personal writing world—which is populated by five novels, five "paranormal" collections, three guidebooks, and two edited volumes—the short stories are sort of a lost tribe, hovering close to extinction. I haven't written any more. The ones that already exist give this collection its title because they are. . . Not Yet Dead.

Hopefully this little book will breathe some new life into them.

❧ Them Bald-headed Snays ❧

After the cancer got Mom, Dad took me way out into the Vermont countryside to live with my grandparents.

"I'll come back for you, Daren," he said. His eyes looked all glassy and sad. I bit my top and bottom lips together so I wouldn't cry when he started home without me. Sure he'd come back, but he didn't say when.

Before that day I'd never seen too much of my grandparents. They'd come to visit us in Providence once, right after Mom got sick. But that was years ago, when I was just a kid. I remember how Dad and Grampa would have long quiet talks that would end suddenly if Mom or me came into the room.

After that they never came to visit again. I don't think Mom liked them, though she never said why. "Their ways are different from ours," that's all she'd say.

And they sure weren't the way I remembered them. Grampa turned out to be sort of strange and a little scary. He was given to long silent stretches in his creaky rocking chair. He'd stare out the window for hours, or read from big, dark-covered books. Sometimes he'd look through the collection of catalogs that seemed to arrive with every mail delivery. My job was to run to the bottom of the hill and pick up the mail from the mailbox. There were always the catalogs, and big brown envelopes with odd designs on them. There were bills, too, and Grampa's once-a-week newspaper. But there was never a letter from Dad.

"Can we call Dad?" I asked. Grampa just snorted as if to say, you know we ain't got a phone. Then he turned away and went back to his reading. Sometimes he'd stand up, take a deep breath, and stretch, reaching way up toward the ceiling. Then he'd walk—maybe to the kitchen—bent over a little, rubbing the lower part of his back.

Grampa didn't talk to me much, but Gram was the quiet one. She'd move from room to room like a draft. Sometimes I'd think I was all alone, then I'd look over my shoulder and Gram would be sitting there, watching me. At first I'd smile at her, but soon I stopped; I'd learned not to expect a smile in return, only a look of concern.

Sometimes she'd bring me a big glass of greenish-brown tea

that tasted of honey and smelled like medicine.

"How you feeling today, Daren?" she'd ask.

"Good," I'd say.

"You drink up, now." She'd nod, pushing the glass toward me. "You'll feel even better."

When I'd take the glass away from my mouth she'd be gone.

Every other Friday Grampa went into town to get groceries. After I'd been there about a month he took me along with him. And that was another odd thing about him: he had a horse and buggy when everybody else had cars. I felt embarrassed riding through the downtown traffic beside an old man in a horse-drawn wagon.

Grampa said his back was acting up real bad so he made me carry all the bags to the wagon. Then he told me to stay put while he made a second stop at the liquor store.

I didn't, though. I took a dime from my pocket and tried to make a collect call to my father. The operator said our number was no longer in service.

Grampa returned with his bottle before I'd made it back to the wagon. He yelled at me; told me he'd tan me brown if I ever disobeyed him again.

I'd lived there in Stockton, Vermont about two months before I saw Bobby Snay.

I was playing in the barn, upstairs in the hayloft, looking out the loading door toward the woods. I saw him come out from among the trees. He swayed as he walked, moving with difficulty, just as if a heavy wind was trying to batter him back to where he'd come from.

He continued across the meadow, weaving through the tall grass and wildflowers until he came to the road that ends in Grampa's dooryard. As he got closer I saw how funny he looked. His skin was the color of marshmallows, his eyes were so pale it was impossible to say if they were blue or brown. And it looked like his hair was falling out.

Maybe it wasn't really falling out, but it wasn't very plentiful. It looked limp and sparse and it stuck out here and there in little patches, making his head look like it was covered with hairy bugs.

Back home he would have been the type of kid we'd pick on in school. But here, well, he was the only other kid I'd seen for a long time.

"Hey!" I called, "Hey! Wait up!"

I dodged back into the barn and jumped down into the pile of hay below. I sneezed once, then made for the door to run after him. But I didn't need to; he was in the barn waiting for me.

All of a sudden I wasn't so eager to say hi. In fact, I was kind of scared of him. He was taller than me, but he was spindly, weak-looking. I wasn't afraid he was going to beat me up or anything. It was something else. Maybe it was the way he had crossed the dooryard and entered the barn in less time than it took me to jump out of the loft. Maybe it was the way he stared at me as if there was no brain behind his washed-out eyes.

Or maybe it was the smell.

I didn't realize it at the time, but now I think that strange odor was coming from him.

It was like the odor of earth, the unfamiliar scent of things that were once alive, like rotting squirrels and leaves, mixed with the smell of things that would never live, like water and stones.

"I... I'm Daren Oakly."

"Bobby," he said. "Bobby Snay." His voice was windy-sounding, like air through a straw.

"Where you going?" I couldn't think of anything else to say.

"Walkin', jes' walkin'. Wanna come?"

"Ah... No. Grampa says I gotta stay here."

"You don't gotta. Nobody gotta. Nobody stays here."

It was warm in the barn. The smell seemed to get stronger.

"Where d'ya live?"

He pointed with his thumb, pointed toward the woods.

"You live in the woods?"

"Yup. Sometimes."

"How old are you?"

He blinked. It seemed strange to see him blink. I hadn't noticed until then, but it was the first time he'd blinked since we stood face to face.

"I gotta go now," he said. "But I'll come again. I always come 'round when ya need me."

I watched him walk away, lurching, leaning, zig-zagging through the field. He had no more than stepped back into the woods when I heard Grampa's wagon coming up the hill.

❧ ❧

"You ain't to do it again," Grampa raged. "I won't have it. I won't have you keepin' time with them bald-headed Snays! Not now, not till I tell ya. You don't know nothin' about 'em, so you stay clear of 'em, hear me?"

"But—"

"You see them around here again, you run an' tell me. That's the long an' short of it."

"But Grampa—!"

It was the fastest I'd ever seen him move. His hand went up like a hammer and came down like a lightning bolt, striking my cheek.

"An' that's so you don't forget."

Anger flared in me; adrenalin surged uselessly. Then fear settled over everything. I couldn't look at Grampa. My nose felt warm. Red drops splatted on the wooden floor like wax from a candle. I bit my lips and fought away the tears.

Later, I heard him telling Gram, "They're back. The boy seen one of 'em just today." Grampa sounded excited — almost happy.

I woke up to the sound of shouting. Outside my bedroom window, near the corner of the barn, two men were fighting. One of them, the one doing the hollering, was Grampa.

"I don't care who you come for. I'm the one's got you now!"

Grampa pushed the other man away, butted him with his shoulder against the open barn door. The door flapped back, struck the side of the building like a thunderclap.

I could see the other man now; it was Bobby Snay.

Grampa hit him in the stomach. Bobby doubled up. Puke shot out of his nose and mouth.

Grampa lifted a boot and Bobby's head jerked back so hard I thought his neck would snap. He tumbled sideways, slid down the barn door and curled up on the ground.

Grampa stomped hard on his head, once, twice. Every time his boot came down he'd yell, "YEH!"

There was a big stone near the barn. Grampa kept it there to hold the door open. It was about the size of a basketball, yet Grampa picked it up like it was weightless.

I couldn't believe how easily Grampa lifted that rock all the way to his shoulders. Then he did something crazy: he let it drop. Bobby lay still after it smashed against his spine.

Grampa turned and walked toward the house. He was smiling.

All the rest of the day I tried to pretend I hadn't seen anything. I knew I couldn't tell Gramma, so I actually tried to forget how weird Grampa was acting. But I couldn't forget; I was too scared of him.

It was then I decided that staying clear of him wouldn't be enough. I'd have to sneak off and run away. Then I'd find my father and things would be pretty much the way they used to be.

Gramma watched me force down a bowl of pea soup at the silent dinner table. Then I got up and started toward the back door. My plan was to run through the woods to the main road, then hitch a ride.

When I opened the door, Grampa was in the yard. He stood tall and straight, hands on hips. That arthritic droop to his shoulders was gone now. His face, though wrinkled as ever, seemed to glow with fresh pulsing blood. He was still smiling.

I knew he could tell by the terror on my face that I'd seen everything. "Get dressed," he said, "you got some work to do."

I thought he was going to make me bury Bobby Snay's body. Instead, he made me go down cellar to stack the firewood he handed to me through a window. We did that all afternoon. After about an hour my back was hurting awful, but Grampa never slowed-up. Now and then he'd stand up straight and stretch his arms wide. He'd smile; sometimes he'd laugh.

I didn't dare say anything to him.

I could hardly eat supper. I was tired and achy and I wanted to take a nap. Grampa wasn't tired at all. He ate lots of beans and biscuits and even carried on a conversation with Gramma. "I feel ten years younger," he said.

The next day Grampa went into town again. I asked him if I could go, too. I wanted to get at least that far in the wagon, then... Well, I wasn't sure. I'd go to the police, or run away, or something.

He said, "No. I'm goin' alone. I want you here."

I was sitting on the fence by the side of the barn trying to decide what to do next when Bobby Snay stepped out of the woods.

I couldn't believe it!

As he got closer, I saw what was really strange: he wasn't bruised or cut or anything. I mean, I was sure Grampa had killed him, but now here he was, without any trace of that awful beating.

He walked closer, weaving this way and that, as if one of his legs was shorter than the other. When he was near enough to hear me, I forced myself to ask, "Are you okay?"

He stopped walking. His eyes were pointed in my direction, but I didn't feel as if he was seeing me. "Yeah," he said, "Yeah sure, 'course I am."

Then he lurched to the right as if someone had shoved him, and he continued on his way.

I watched him go, not believing, not knowing.

Should I tell Grampa Bobby was okay? Should I talk to the law? Keep quiet? Or what? I had to decide; I had to do something.

Friday at supper Gramma had a heart attack.

She was spooning stew onto Grampa's plate when she dropped the pot. Grampa's hand went up just like he was going to smack her. Then he saw what was happening.

She put both her hands on the table top, trying to steady herself. Her knuckles were white. Sweat popped out all over her face. "I... I... I...," she said, as if her tongue was stuck on that one word.

Then her knees folded and she dropped to the floor.

Grampa said, "Jesus, oh Jesus... oh God." But instead of bending over and helping Gramma, he did something awful weird: he grabbed his shotgun and ran out the door.

Left alone with Gramma, I didn't know what to do. I knelt over her and tried to ask her how I could help. I was crying so hard I was afraid she couldn't understand what I was saying.

Now her skin had turned completely white; her lips looked blue. Her whole face was shiny with sweat. She whispered something: "Go get me a Snay, boy. Go quick."

I didn't argue. I ran toward the door.

Maybe Mr. Snay was a doctor or a preacher or something, I didn't know. Whatever he was, Gramma wanted to see him. She seemed to need him. Somehow, I guessed, he'd be able to help her.

Quickly finding the path Bobby Snay had taken earlier, I entered the woods. Almost at once, I heard noises. Grunting sounds. Soft thupps. Cracks and groans.

It was Grampa and one of the Snays—not Bobby this time, but surely one of his relatives. It was a girl. She had the same tall, frail body, the same mushroom-white complexion, the same patchy growths of hair.

Grampa was smashing her with a piece of pipe that looked like a tire iron. The Snay didn't fight back, didn't scream, she just stood there taking the blows. I saw Grampa jab at her with the flattened end of the metal rod. It went right through her eye, sinking half-way into her skull. She fell backwards, sat on the ground. Grampa jerked the rod up and down just like he was pumping the blood that spurted from her eye socket.

I couldn't look but I couldn't run away. "Grampa," I shouted, "stop it! You gotta help Gramma!"

Grampa finished what he was doing and looked up. His eyes were fierce, fiery-looking. Then he took a step toward me, squeezing the bloody pipe in his slimy red hand.

He looked wild.

I backed away from him, thinking, he's going to brain me with that thing.

Then my heel hit something.

The shotgun!

I picked it up from where Grampa must have dropped it. I guessed he wanted to do this job by hand. I guessed he enjoyed it.

I pointed the gun at Grampa.

"Put that down boy!" His voice was as gruff as I'd ever heard it. When he stepped toward me I stepped backward, almost stumbled. I had the gun, but that didn't keep me from being afraid.

"Put it down." He waved the tire iron, gesturing for me to drop the shotgun. Tears blurred my vision; the gun shook in my hands.

"Listen to me boy...." His hand was reaching out.

I looked around. The Snay wasn't moving. There was no one to help me.

Grampa took another step.

"I'm tellin' you, boy—"

Closer.

I cried out and pulled the trigger.

If I hadn't been shaking so much I might have killed him straight off. As it was, his shirt tore away and red slimy skin exploded from his left side.

We both fell at the same time, me from the recoil, Grampa from the buckshot.

I looked at him. A white, red-glazed hip-bone showed through his mangled trousers. Broken ribs like teeth bit through the shredded flesh.

"Daren," he said. This time his voice was weak.

I couldn't move. I couldn't go to him. I couldn't run away.

"Daren, you don't understand nothin'."

I could barely hear him. "The Snay's," he said. "You gotta give 'em your pain. You gotta give 'em your troubles. You can't hurt 'em. You can't kill 'em. They jest keep comin' back...."

I found myself on my feet again, moving closer to Grampa, dragging the shotgun by the barrel.

Suddenly, I was standing above him.

"You shot me, boy, but you can make it right. You gotta do one of 'em, boy. You gotta do jes' like you're killin' one of 'em. Then I'll be all right. You gotta kill one of 'em for me."

"But what about Gramma—?"

"Please, boy..." His voice was weak. I could barely hear him.

He lifted his finger toward the Snay with the ruined eye. "See that. I got to her in time. Your Gramma's all right."

I needed proof. I wanted to run back to the house to see for myself, but there was no time. And Grampa was dying.

The mangled Snay was moving now. She was using the tree trunk to work her way back up to her feet.

"See there, boy," Grampa wheezed. "Get her boy, shoot her. Hit her with the gun!"

I lifted the shotgun, braced my shoulder for another recoil.

"Hurry Daren, 'fore she gets away."

My finger touched the trigger. I was shaking so much the metal seemed to vibrate against my fingertip.

"Please, boy..." Grampa was propped up on his elbow. He watched the Snay lurch and stumble into the shadowy trees—

"Now, boy, NOW!"

—and disappear.

Grampa collapsed on to the ground. He was flat on his back, his head rested on an exposed root. Now his eyes were all cloudy-looking. They slid around in different directions.

I was still posed with the gun against my shoulder. When he tried to speak again, I let it fall to the ground.

I had to kneel down, put my ear right up next to his mouth, to hear what he was saying.

"You shoulda shot, Daren—"

"I couldn't, Grampa." I was blubbering. "I can't shoot nobody..." My tears fell and splattered on Grampa's face.

"You gotta, son. Your daddy, he never had no stomach for it neither. Couldn't even do it to save your mama. That's why he brung you here. He knew old Gramp would know what to do. That cancer that got your mamma, boy, that cancer that killed her. Well Daren, you got it, too."

His words stopped in a gag, his eyes froze solid, and he was dead.

I looked up. Looked around. The Snay was gone. The birds were quiet. I was alone in the woods.

❧ Penetration ❧

He hadn't meant to hit her so hard.

Even now, after all this time, his right hand still tingled as if a low electrical current were pulsing through it.

But damn, if she wasn't always bitching about everything, they'd get along fine. God, it was as if Vicki thought that Christly marriage license entitled her to unlimited nagging rights. If he wasn't earning money, if he weren't providing, that would be one thing. But his job selling drugs for Shodale Laboratories earned them plenty: enough to have bought a $400,000 condo on the lake, enough so he and Vicki had talked about having a baby.

Maybe he should call to apologize. He wanted to talk to her; he wanted to make sure she was okay. But if she started in on him again he'd hang up and head downstairs to the bar.

That was the trouble with life on the road. No matter where he stayed, hotel, motel, or bed and breakfast, there was always a tavern and a little good-natured company just a short walk away.

Hell, she should try it sometime. She should spend twenty-five to thirty weeks a year in cars, on planes and in look-alike hotel rooms. A few months of that and she'd be hitting the bars, too.

As it was they spent so little time together you'd think she'd back off and give him some breathing room. Maybe be glad to see him once in a while.

"Look at yourself," she had railed at him, "home less than twenty-four hours and already you're half passed out in front of the damn television. You got no substance, Jason. You're weak, you're irresponsible. Why most men would want to be doing things with their wife, not just sitting around guzzling bourbon and channel surfing. God, Jason, you're an alcoholic. I married a goddamn drunk!"

What happened after that was a little fuzzy. He remembered the screams more than the specific words that she'd screamed. There was something about not being solid enough, not the way a married man's supposed to be. He'd shot something back and she'd told him to go to hell. That much he remembered for sure. "You go straight to hell, Jason Tanner!"

And he remembered smacking her. Not hard. Not with his fist, but with his open hand, just the way he always did. Just to warn her.

And he remembered her falling.

Next thing Jason knew he was driving away. He had to be in Vermont tomorrow anyway; he had a presentation at that little clinic in Burlington. So he'd checked into the hotel a day early. So what? He could expense account it with no trouble.

And now, sitting in front of the TV, he still couldn't relax. Mostly because of her, he couldn't relax.

Yes. It was Vicki's fault, not his. So why should he call to apologize?

She should call him.

But she didn't know where he was staying. And that was just the way he planned to keep it. In fact, maybe he should just take off, disappear. Never come back. Let her do a little of the worrying for once.

He'd think about it. But for now he'd go out. Find some company. Have a couple of drinks. Maybe then he could relax.

The buzz of the alarm clock was like an annoying mosquito. Jason swatted at it, trying to hit the snooze button. Instead he knocked a half-filled glass of bourbon to the floor. The soft pile of the carpet kept it from breaking.

He swatted again. Damn. Can't find the snooze button.

With his head pounding as if a wrecking ball were slamming against his skull, Jason opened his eyes, squinted at the clock.

Maybe there was no snooze alarm.

No. It's there. A recessed brown button on the right hand corner of the clock radio. They couldn't have made it any harder to see. Or to push.

Jason reached over, took aim, and let his extended forefinger drop like a bomb towards its target.

Bingo!

But the buzzing didn't stop.

Why... What the—?

He jerked his hand away. Not believing.

No.

No.

That couldn't have happened. No way. Still, what he thought he'd seen jolted him wide awake, his headache forgotten.

Now, sitting on the side of the bed, he tried it again. With his extended finger poised over the snooze alarm, he focused on the half-inch gap between fingertip and button. Then he lowered the finger, closing the gap. The alarm continued to sound; the finger continued to descend. It was as if the button's surface had turned to liquid. His finger passed right through it, sinking all the way to the knuckle.

Mouth hanging open, eyes wide, Jason stared in disbelief as he slid his finger deeper into the radio. It was not an unpleasant sensation. It felt warm, that's all; the whole length of his finger seemed to heat up. Then he felt a flush of heat spread over his whole body. Must be some kind of physiological reaction to unreality, he thought, yanking his finger out fast.

He took a couple of deep breaths, felt his heart thumping.

Once more, he thought, once more just to be sure...

Cautiously, he repeated the penetration, slower this time, more deliberate.

There was a slight sensation of pressure as his skin made contact with the plastic button. Then, as he pushed, he could feel the heat again. Not hot. Not uncomfortable in any way. Jason suspected it was caused by atoms rearranging within his flesh as they slipped between the atoms of the radio. But that was just a guess. Physics was never his best subject.

Uncertain that he was truly awake, Jason studied his finger, buried in the radio to the second joint. It looked like a white worm crawling into a hole. He slid it up and down, afraid it might stick there if he let it rest. It moved easily—in... out—as if the radio were made of butter.

Jason removed his finger and held it up to his eyes, examining it. It was slightly red around the knuckle. When he touched it he could feel warmth.

Next he tried knocking on the radio, tapping it with his fist. A proper tattoo sounded when his knuckles rapped the button and surrounding plastic. The alarm stopped buzzing.

He tried the penetration again, this time using the forefinger on his opposite hand.

Nothing. Solid as granite.

So he tried all his other fingers, one at a time, in combinations. No good. The problem was just that one finger, the index finger of his right hand.

Jason tensed, thinking. The impossibility of the experience was paralyzing. As he articulated it in his mind, trying to describe what had happened, he couldn't bring himself to believe it. He had actually pushed his finger through a solid object.

Nope. No way. That can't happen.

But it did.

Weird, he thought. Too freaking weird.

Was the fault with the radio or his finger? To find out he focused on the bedside table. He'd try a test. Jason dropped his extended finger onto the brown fake wood grain of the tabletop. It slipped through with no more difficulty than pushing it into warm mud.

Leaving it embedded, he dragged himself a little higher on the mattress so he could peer underneath the table. Sure enough, he could see a fleshy protuberance on the lower side.

I'm dreaming, he thought. This. Just. Can't. Be.

Sweat rained from his forehead as he pulled his trembling hand away. His underarms leaked like faucets as he stretched out on his bed, trying to relax.

Thinking back, Jason recalled that he had often poked things with that same finger—a doorbell, the shoulder of a friend, a smudge on his sunglasses —but his finger had never penetrated anything before.

He lifted his left hand to his face, positioning it so his thumb pointed toward his nose. He brought his right hand up beside it, index finger extended, aimed at his palm.

I wonder, he thought. I wonder....

Very carefully he touched his right forefinger to the center of his left palm.

Slowly, ever so slowly, he pushed.

He watched his finger sinking into his flesh. Now the nail was buried within the palm. The folds of skin on the first joint disappeared as the nail emerged on the other side. And now the second joint slipped through.

But the process stopped at his knuckle. That was it. That was as far as it would go. The knuckle remained solid.

He separated his hands and let his arms fall to his sides. He felt strangely exhausted. After closing his eyes he thought about it. Somehow... Somehow his finger had lost its solidity. How could such a thing be?

He woke up convinced the whole thing had been a dream. His headache was gone and a glance at the clock told him it was almost noon.

He reached out and touched the top of his bedside table. Nothing. Surely the bizarre events had been part of a drunken nightmare.

After a shower and shave he dressed hurriedly and took the elevator down to The Garden Cafe where he ordered soup and a sliced turkey sandwich. He wasn't really hungry, but he felt oddly weak. And tired. Of course that wasn't unusual after a night of serious boozing.

He thought of his wife. Her surprised expression and the slap's impact had burned themselves into his memory. Yes, after lunch he would go back to his room and phone her. They both knew it was part of a pattern, but—now that he was sober and somewhat rested—he really did feel horrible about having hit her. He felt horrible every time he hit her.

When the waiter placed the bowl of soup in front of him, Jason discovered he couldn't pick up his spoon. His finger slipped RIGHT THROUGH it as if the utensil were fabricated from smoke. The spoon clattered on the table when it connected with a solid part of his hand: the surface of his thumb.

Feeling the heat of fear sear through him, Jason looked around wondering if anyone had seen. He wasn't going to be able to eat! Not without making a spectacle of himself. He imagined having to put his face right down to the chicken noodle soup and slurping like a dog in order to take in any nourishment. The thought embarrassed him and suddenly he wasn't hungry anymore.

Using his left hand, he tried to slide the soup away from him. His thumb and forefinger penetrated the ceramic bowl, coming to rest within the hot soup. He cried out, flicking his scalded fingers. Automatically, he lifted them to his mouth. His lips closed around them and met, his solid seeming digits less tangible than vapor.

People were looking at him now, reacting to his startled cry. Jason fled from the room, knowing he wouldn't be able to sign for his lunch.

He had to hit the elevator button with his elbow.

As he sped down the hall toward his room, Jason knew he needed help. He had to call someone, but who? Most people would say a psychiatrist; they'd think he was imagining this impossible affliction. But a psychiatrist wouldn't know any more than he did about what was happening.

Maybe he should call a doctor. It was possible he had contracted some weird new disease. Maybe some unheard of contagion had started at his fingertip and was spreading through his whole body. Perhaps some undiscovered form of flesh-eating virus?

Hey! If it really was an illness, maybe he already had something to treat it among the drug samples in the trunk of his car.

No. That was stupid. Too hit or miss. What he needed was some kind of scientist. A physicist, somebody who knew about matter.

All Jason remembered was that matter existed in three forms: solid, liquid, and gas. Each form was made up of atoms which in turn were made up of tinier particles. Supposedly a lot of nothingness existed between those tiny particles. In theory, he supposed, it was possible for one solid object to penetrate another if the particles of one could somehow pass through the nothingness of the other.

Yes, theoretically, it was possible.

Theoretically? Hell, it was real. Christ, it was happening to him!

Standing in front of the door to his room, Jason gripped the handle. His hand, like the hand of a ghost, passed right through it. He had to push it down with his elbow. When he did, the material of his coat sleeve collapsed like an empty sock.

God, the condition was spreading. It had moved from his hands right up his arms!

If he couldn't turn the handle, he surely couldn't fish his room key out of his pocket. There was no way in the world he could get back into his room!

"I've locked myself out," he said to a maid pushing past with her cleaning cart. "Would you mind letting me in?"

"Certainly, sir."

She unlocked the door and held it open for him. No doubt she expected a tip. Impossible, Jason knew. He dismissed her with a "Thank you."

Sitting on the edge of his bed, Jason felt desperate to phone Vicki. She had to come here. She had to help him. He'd apologize if he had to; he'd say anything it took. He just couldn't stand to be alone right now. And he couldn't—he simply couldn't —tell anyone what was happening to him.

Jason reached for the telephone. His fingers disappeared into the receiver where they closed into a fist.

The realization was excruciating.

Something had changed.

Something was horribly wrong.

Suddenly he was no longer a drug salesman. Christ, he couldn't even pick up his sample case.

Now he had become... something else. Something alien.

But what?

A candidate for the "strange-but-true" books, right along with fire eaters, human pincushions and people who could bend spoons just by thinking about it. Suddenly he was a carnival freak: Jason Tanner, The Man Who Can Walk Through Walls!

Through walls...?

Could he really?

Giggling, Jason decided that would be his next experiment.

He stepped into the bathroom, one wall of which was a floor to ceiling mirror.

He giggled again.

The combined weight of his sport coat and shirt had pushed down through his shoulders. Now a ridge of material sort of bisected his torso. He was stark naked from the solar plexus up.

That confirmed what was happening. Little by little, a section at a time, his body was becoming incorporeal. It was as if he were turning from a solid to a gas.

That's what I'll call myself, Jason chuckled. Gasman. I'll have the greatest act on the midway!

He stared at himself as, slowly, his clothing sank farther and farther down through the intangible mass of his body. He watched it descend. Jason was turning to gas more rapidly now. And— as they say on the midway—right before his very eyes! Soon the jacket, shirt, pants and underwear had pooled at his feet. He stepped out of them.

He used one shoe to pry off the other. Then he stepped on the toe of his sock and pulled it off.

Soon Jason stood naked before the bathroom mirror.

He didn't look any different. He looked heavy. Solid. Fat.

I wonder if I can penetrate the mirror? he thought. I wonder if I can follow Alice through the looking glass?

He was standing just two feet from the glass. Focusing on the reflection of his nose, he extended his right index finger. It met its double at the mirror's surface. The nail, fleshy ridges of the first joint, and finally the rest of his finger vanished into the glass. His hand followed.

He did the same with his other hand. Now he and his twin were joined by two long, handless arms. More than ever he looked like a candidate for the freak show—a grotesque set of Siamese twins, joined at both wrists.

He stepped forward. His arms sank to a point beyond the elbows. He tried to link invisible fingers together on the far side of the wall, but could feel only a vague ripple of heat as one hand passed through the other.

Now, with his nose almost touching the nose of his reflection, Jason began to lose his nerve. Something about the idea of pushing his head into the glass really frightened him.

Looking down, peering over the hairy mound of his belly, he could see the tips of both big toes buried in the mirror. He pressed his stomach against the hard, cold surface. His belly didn't flatten. Instead it seemed to merge with its bloated clone.

The whole front of his body felt as if it were slightly sunburned: warm from the melding of the atoms, but not painful.

Still looking down, he allowed his forehead to come in contact with the glass wall. Penetration was very like lowering his face into bath water. He could feel an almost pleasant warming as his forehead sank into its reflection. In his imagination he pictured the convoluted gray mass of his brain seeping through the molecules of glass.

Jason altered his balance just a bit, leaned ever so slightly forward, effortlessly melding with the glass. He suspected the entire length of his body was actually bisected by the plane of the mirror. He could do it! He could actually walk through the wall! Jason prepared to slide his feet forward another inch, but found he could not. He couldn't force them through. Movement stopped at the base of his toes. Apparently his solid-to-vapor transformation wasn't complete. Apparently it hadn't spread to his feet.

He stepped back, pulled out, faced his reflection in the polished glass. He was naked. Barefoot. He looked pale and he suddenly felt terribly weak. Perhaps, he reasoned, penetrating objects requires a lot of energy. I should eat something. I should rest, he thought.

But, he realized, that would be impossible. No bed would support him. And how could he eat?

Another realization shocked him: What if his feet changed? God, he might soon be sinking into the floor, his feet dangling through the ceiling of the room below.

With that, panic coursed through him like a surge of electricity. Wasting no time he turned from the mirror and rushed back into his room. He made a swipe for his trench coat but couldn't grasp it. ...what if he sank into the floor...?

Jesus! He had to get out of here! His hotel room was three stories up!

Jason ran to the door but his hand couldn't grip the handle.

Then he suddenly realized, he didn't need to open it!

He tried stepping through the door—a woman in the hall spotted him and screamed—but his solid ankles locked against the wood, tripping him. He pitched through the wooden barrier, plunging face first toward the carpet of the hall.

He connected with the floor and kept on falling.

Suddenly he was hanging upside-down, suspended by his ankles, dangling from the ceiling of the room below like an inverted human chandelier. A fat old man was sitting in a chair puffing a cigar and watching the Oprah show.

"Help me!" Jason cried.

The man looked up. His face twisted into a horrified knot. He started to rise, gasping, "Ah, ah, aaaah...." Pudgy hands leaped to his heaving chest, clutched the material of his robe. The cigar tumbled from his mouth as he sank to the carpet.

"Help!" Jason cried. "Help! Help!"

His left foot let go.

Then the right.

And he was falling.

Instinctively Jason pulled his hands to his face, defending against impact with the floor. But it was unnecessary. He dropped like a contorting swimmer tumbling headfirst into a pool. But the carpeted floor offered less resistance than water.

He shot into another room, hoping something would break his fall, but he kept falling.

Down through a dark banquet room.

A dimly lighted basement with pipes and boilers.

Then darkness.

Solid earth. Jason plummeted through the ground itself.

In some sane part of his mind he knew he was at the mercy of gravity. And when gravitational forces equalized, his fall would end.

Somewhere near the center of the earth.

The molten center of the earth.

Already he could feel things getting warmer.

❧ Soul Keeper ❧

The door was unlocked. He was sure of it. The old man had never turned the key!

Carl pressed his ear against its heavy wooden panels, listening. He touched the painted oak with his fingertips, touched the lock, the hinge, the frame itself, feeling for vibrations. Listening...

Did he dare to open it?

No! It could be a trick. The old man might be waiting on the other side with a knife or a gun.

But that wasn't right. Carl had clearly heard him descend the stairs, his heavy footfalls unmistakable as they faded. And he hadn't come back up; Carl had been listening for hours. God, it must be almost midnight by now.

Eyes closed, forehead against the door, Carl tried to remember how things had looked on the other side. He could recall the narrow unlighted stairway leading to the hall below. Was there carpet on the stairs? He didn't know; he just couldn't remember.

And what of the downstairs hall? Was it carpeted? Was the floor exposed wood and potentially noisy? Would he have to walk in his stocking feet so as not to be heard?

If he were lucky, he could make it down the stairs, across the hall, and to the safety of the outside. But wait; if he got out, he'd need his shoes. Trouble was, if he carried them, he'd have only one hand free to defend himself.

God, there were so many little details. Any one of them could mean the difference between life and death.

Carl took the doorknob in his hand, moved it minutely to the left and right. Did he dare?

Listening...

Quiet on the other side. He sensed no vibration with his fingertips, heard nothing with his fine-tuned ears. All was still. Even the relentless squall of the televangelists was silenced for another day.

The old man must be in bed.

But was he sleeping?

Carl stood up. His back, still stiff from the accident, protested with a dull tug of pain. "Ahhh!" But his wounded leg was better; the swelling was down. Finally, he was able to bend it at the knee. He was certain he could walk on it with no trouble.

But could he run?

What if the old man heard him? Or saw him?

What if he had to run?

Would he be able to?

And how far?

It didn't matter; it was worth the risk. If he didn't leave tonight, now, he might be doomed to remain a captive in this tiny prison for another week, a month, maybe longer. In fact, he might never get another crack at escape. He'd have to wait—months maybe—until the old man forgot to lock the door again.

No. Now was the time. By God, he'd risk it.

His fingers tightened on the cold doorknob and—he took a deep breath—turned it.

Thank God! It really was unlocked! Oh, thank God.

Now, the problem was immediate. And simple. Could he open the door quietly, descend the stairs, make it all the way to the front door without waking the old man?

He didn't know; he wasn't confident.

Feeling the punch of his heart against the inside of his chest, Carl willed himself to be calm.

I'd better take another minute and think.

He had to remember everything, to picture precisely all the features of the old house. He wanted to anticipate every obstacle between here and freedom. Were there irregularities in the walls? Would he find furniture blocking his way in the darkness? Did the outside door open outward, or inward? He had to remember, he had to...

His life depended on it.

Carl sat down on the carpet, his back to the door, and, for the millionth time, he ran through all of it in his memory.

The First Day

The fight with Lucy had been a stupid thing. Tithing for Christ sake! Now she wanted him to pledge twenty percent of his income to the church! Twenty percent!

"You're the one who 'got religion,' but I'm the one who's paying for it!"

Her eyes did their best Tammy Bakker imitation, filling quickly
with sparkling tears. It was as if her pudgy body were sculpted from
a wet sponge, and he was squeezing it.

His anger rose as he scanned their checkbook. April third,
check number 215 paid to The Church of the Christian Soldiers,
fifteen dollars. April tenth, twenty-five dollars. April 17, twenty-five
dollars. Good God, he only earned $304.00 a week at the gas station!
There was the rent, the car payments, Jilly's braces. Christ, there
was food to buy!

"You're already giving away twenty-five dollars a week! Do you
know how long it takes me to earn twenty-five dollars? Jesus, Lucy,
we can't afford your religion!"

Her mouth opened. Her right hand fluttered up to her chest,
perched like a dove upon her heart. She took a step backward. "I... I..."

Carl threw the check book at her. Though it missed her head by
inches, it must have triggered her "ON" switch. "You're a Godless
man, Carl Congdon. A Godless, selfish man. There are them whose
need is greater than ours, there are them who..."

Her voice trailed off to a blessed whisper as he slammed the
screen door and stomped across the rain-drenched yard to the car.

"You're bound for damnation, Carl Congdon," she called after
him. "You're bound . . ."

The engine roared when he turned the key. His foot stomped
mercilessly on the accelerator. Burning rubber in reverse, he
screeched into the road, hit the clutch, the shift, and rocketed
northward.

At first there were only a few other cars on the road. Then none
at all. It was too dark, too rainy. Drops of water flattening against
the windshield made the whole world look like it was wrapped in
cellophane.

He took a moment to breathe deeply, willing himself to be
calm. The best medicine, he knew, was tucked into the upholstered
pocket behind the passenger's seat. He reached back—"Ah, got
it!"—and pulled the pint to a place where it would be more useful.
Momentarily taking his hands from the wheel, he removed the cap
and kissed the bottle.

Leaving East Burke and heading toward Burke Hollow, Carl
started to relax. The Vermont hills, day or night, always made him

feel better. God, he thought, her holy-rolling is getting way out of hand. She's gone crazy with it. I never gambled on something like that when I said for better or for worse.

He knew he had about a hundred dollars in his pocket, the money he'd been stashing away to buy Floyd Blount's Harley. "Fuck the Harley," he said out loud. "By Jesus, I'm going to Canada!"

With those simple words Carl had completely severed all the rotting fibers that joined him to his wife and family. It was over. Period. It was just that simple. The Lord could have her.

He continued north, drifting away from the better-traveled routes and on to the narrow pitted traces that criss-crossed Vermont's Northeast Kingdom like lines in the palm of a hand. The Kingdom was the most remote, least settled part of the state. The forests were vast, the roads were gravel, and the inhabitants were few and far between. As long as he headed north he'd be fine; he was in no hurry. He could be in Montreal before morning.

Trying to recap the pint, he lifted his hands from the wheel. Briefly. Just long enough to drift onto the soft-shoulder of the dirt road. The engine roared as his wheels spat sand and fought for purchase. Wet saplings, resisting the metallic intrusion, swatted at the car as it bore into the bushes.

The last thing he saw was a tree rushing at him. God, it was going to hit—

The Second Day

Eyes.

Two eyes floated before him, staring from out of a mysterious undulating fog. They were like twin headlights in an infinite darkness.

A blink brought the man into focus—the man the eyes belonged to. Dressed in white... must be a doctor.

Carl shook his head trying to wake up. The motion hurt. The fog swirled and throbbed and parted.

He was in a room. Not a hospital room. It was like a library with books on long shelves made of dark wood. Carl could smell those books; they had a musty odor like the magazines he used to read in the barn when he was a boy.

"You have been sent to me," said the man with the eyes, his voice a whisper. The moving lips were barely visible amid the gray thatch of his beard. "You are in my care now. I hope you are feeling better."

It must be a hospital?

The accident rushed back, filling his mind. The tree charging his car—

Remembering the impact shocked Carl to full alertness. Fog cleared as if blasted by sunlight.

It took a moment to find his voice, "Where... where am I?"

The eyes squinted, but didn't close. "You are at my house, high in the sky." The voice had a sing-song quality that Carl didn't like. "Our Good Lord directed me to the wreckage of your vehicle on the road. It is fortunate you were thus chosen. No one would have found you. No one passes that way. And you were suffering, so I brought you here."

"Well... I... thank you, but—"

"No, don't thank me. It is my calling." Then the eyes widened to an unsettling fullness, "You're dead, you know."

Carl's nervous system seized-up like a disc brake. Dead! He flexed his toes, his fingers. Other than the pounding in his head he could feel no pain, no discomfort.

"Dead?" He gulped, his throat dry. "What are you talking about?"

The old man's face, a bird's nest of hair and wrinkles, rearranged itself into a soothing smile. "You are but one step from the Heavenly Land—"

"Now wait a minute!" Carl sat up with a start. The sudden motion hammered in his temples. Settling back on the leather sofa, he waited for the pain to pass.

"W... what do you mean I'm... dead?"

The old man patted Carl's shoulder. He spoke like a stern parent, "My son, your life ended in the wreckage of your car on the road. Until you are finally at peace, it is my calling to make your time in transition—be it days, weeks, or even years—as pleasant for you as possible."

Carl studied the robed, long-haired figure. Only one word came to mind: crazy.

"I... What are you talking about?"

The ancient eyes were patient. "Your final reward, my son. Your days of peace. Come with me, let me show you."

Carl's fleeting thoughts of a fast escape ended when he saw a gun in the old man's hand.

"To where?" Carl said hopelessly, gazing at the barrel of the weapon.

"Why up, of course. Up to Heaven."

With the muzzle of the .38, the bearded man nudged Carl up a narrow, unlit stairway. Carl's back was so tense and numb that any attempt to straighten it resulted in sharp tearing pain. With every step, his injured leg shot bolts of electrical agony along his stooped spine.

At the top of the stairway Carl saw a huge wooden door, painted gold. They opened the heavy door, passed through, and into a foyer that connected four rooms. Carl looked around. This floor, like the one below, showed many indications of the old man's wealth.

Carl scanned the impressive paintings on the walls: sunny pastures, proud white stallions, ships under full sail. There were other pictures too, violent Biblical scenes with scarlet skies and sharp fingers of lightning that pinned wriggling sinners to an endless wall of skulls. There was a portrait of the smiling Jesus and behind him a white bearded deity with merciless maniacal eyes.

Carl shivered. When his gaze came to rest on the hand-carved woodwork framing a nearby window, he gasped. His nerves flared at what he saw behind the glass: bars! They were so black they seemed like part of the night.

A soft sob of dread escaped his heaving lungs.

Carl couldn't pull his unwilling eyes from those bars as the old man continued, "Here you will have everything you may require to make your brief stay comfortable and pleasant. There is an excellent library—I've personally selected the titles. There is a color television set tuned to inspirational programming. And of course stereophonic equipment of rare and unmatched quality. Should there be anything not provided, you may make me aware of it in your prayers. I am a wealthy man, sir. Our Lord has generously provided for me to perform my special calling. I will provide for you just as generously. After all, it is your reward, is it not?

"My reward?"

"Yes my son, you have attained the Heavenly Land. Your stay in transition will be brief. I must prepare you for your journey to the final realm. And now sir, you must rest." The old man smiled beatifically. "Bless you, and good night."

Carl could not speak as he watched the heavy door close. He heard the solid sound of wood against wood. He heard the metal key turn in the lock. "Heaven..." he sighed, "with a big fat lock on the pearly gates."

The Third Day

After the initial panic, after he'd had a little time to think, Carl began to realize the seriousness of his position. Gazing out the barred windows for hours had shown him how far away from civilization he was. All he could see were rolling pine-topped hills, distant pastures, and far, far away to the south, what appeared to be a stream. He couldn't even see a road! Suppose he could figure a way out of here, how would he make his way back to civilization?

The alternative was apparently what the crazy old man had in mind: to hold him prisoner in this ersatz Heaven until he died of old age, or maybe worse, became as loony as his captor.

Carl had a clear idea what religious excess could do to the mind. He had seen the beginnings of some kind of mania in his wife Lucy. Helplessly, he had watched it take hold of her during the eighth year of their marriage. How quickly its stern hands had molded her, transforming her into a self-righteous stranger ping-ponging between frequent fits of scolding and hysterical tears.

Well, he had run away from Lucy, and he could run away from this lunatic as well.

But the time was not right.

Although his back pain had diminished, his leg was still stiff and sore. At first he had feared a fracture, but now he was convinced it was merely a sprain. In any event, running was out of the question. While he waited for it to heal, he would plan his escape.

He knew the bars on the windows and the heavy bolted door would be problems. Perhaps his only hope was to somehow subdue the old man and make a run for it. It wouldn't be easy; the old man never appeared without a Bible in one hand and a weapon in the other.

Two days worth of "classes" had given Carl plenty of insight into the old man's delusions. Apparently he thought he was "God's Man," a modern day prophet charged with the responsibility of preparing near-worthy souls for their ascent into the Second Heaven.

The First Heaven, the old man had explained, was the top floor of his house.

"Our Great God placed you into my hands," the old man was always quick to remind him. "He says you are nearly ready, but yet imperfect. That is why He did not take you in the crash. That is why He entrusted you to me. I shall put the final touches on your salvation."

The old man went on with his sermon as Carl's mind wandered. Vaguely, he heard resonant tones rendering passages from a book the old man had written. A book he'd added to the Bible between the Old and New Testaments. He called it, "The Book of Transition." Carl had to fight tears of resignation with every lofty sounding phrase.

The same brutal realization hit him again and again: he was being held by a madman, and there was absolutely nothing he could do about it.

He feigned attention and dreamed of escape.

Today's "Lesson" consisted of a few confusing remarks intended to clarify the Bible readings. The concluding statement showcased the prophet's skills as an orator, "Those of us placed above temptation are nearer yet to the Golden Light. All men must be guided by the prophet, as the wisdom of the prophet is guided by the Light. Yield not to temptation, for those who embrace its worldly rewards will never attain the Heavenly Land, and all will be lost."

The old man paused dramatically, looking at his congregation of one. He punctuated the lesson's end with a stiff nod of the head, then he left the room. His long black cassock flapped behind him like the wings of a crow.

In the silence that followed, Carl heard the familiar sound of the key turning in the lock.

He stared at the barred window and he wept.

The Fifth Day

His breakfast tray did not arrive. Noon came and passed, but there was no midday meal.

Could something have happened to the old man?

Carl's brief flash of hope quickly turned into a new terror: if the old man died or took off, Carl could waste away and starve to death. He ran to the golden door. Tried it. Found it locked. He pounded until his hands throbbed and hollered till his throat was hoarse. Nothing.

Then he ran to the window and shouted some more.

Exhausted, sobbing, Carl settled into a fitful nap. When he awoke, his dinner tray was on the table in the foyer. It was empty except for a note on his pewter plate. It said:

One must learn to accept God's gifts with an attitude of restraint and moderation.

For today's lesson, you must learn the glory of self-denial.

The Fifteenth Day

By now Carl was convinced the old man was planning to kill him.

He suspected that when he had learned the lessons to the old man's satisfaction, a bullet to the head—or something equally lethal—would propel him the rest of the way into Heaven.

Or maybe it would be nothing so rapid. He knew the once-a-day oatmeal was not enough to sustain him much longer. Was he fated to starve to death?

From somewhere he remembered a saying he had once heard, something about those who God will destroy He'd first make mad.

Well, madness was close at hand. He found himself praying that the bodily destruction to follow would be mercifully swift. A quick bullet to the brain would be preferable to this gradual starvation.

God, he was so weak; he slept ten to fourteen hours a day. His health and his sanity seemed to be draining away. Death. Sleep. Insanity. Anything would be preferable to another week of this imprisonment.

Death was beginning to seem like a friend.

The Twenty-First Day

Carl awoke on the floor when something jabbed his head. He opened his eyes. The shades in the room were drawn; it would have been completely black but for the light of the television. A profusely sweating Reverend Mercy paraded back and forth on the screen; luckily the sound was off.

Something jabbed Carl's head again. Eyes shifting left, he saw the old man kneeling beside him, poking his temple with the muzzle of the pistol.

"Hey!" Carl protested.

"Shhhh," said the old man. "It's time for our lesson."

As Carl started to get up he realized one foot was chained to the floor. "What's this? Why'd you do that?"

"Today you must learn to humble yourself before the Lord." There was repressed thunder in the old man's voice.

Carl was on his feet now. The eighteen inch length of chain made walking impossible.

"Now you must kneel before the Lord!" The voice was loud, commanding. The eyes blazed with an unworldly light. "On your knees, sinner. On your knees and ask the good Lord to take you home."

Carl felt the strength drain from his legs. His knees turned to Jell-O. Weakened by irregular meals and the drugs he was convinced the old man was giving him, Carl took care not to fall. But even in such an unrelenting state of fear, he'd be damned if he'd kneel before this lunatic.

"On your knees before me!"

"I won't."

The old man pushed Carl off balance. The chain stiffened, snagged his untethered foot. He toppled, his face smashed against the wooden floor.

"On your knees. Now. Or know the vengeance of the Light."

A sob squeezed from his constricted throat.

Carl shifted his position, got one knee firmly under him before lifting himself onto both.

The Final Day

Carl feigned sleep there on the floor, pretending he'd passed out. The events which immediately followed were like the short precise acts of a tragic play: he felt the old man remove the chain, stomp to the door, unlock it, pull it open, close it, and descend the stairs.

He heard every footfall.

Only then did he dare to open his eyes. The room was surreal in the unearthly blue light from the TV screen. Rain beat against the window glass.

Carl crawled to the sofa and tried to pull himself up. The chain was gone but the skin around his ankle was raw and bleeding. His wounded leg throbbed.

When he was able to get to his feet, he walked unsteadily from room to room. He wanted to limber up and to make sure he was alone.

As always, in an automatic part of his wandering ritual, he listened at the door to the stairway. Then, absently, he tried it.

Unlocked!

He couldn't believe it!

In his rage the old man had forgotten to secure the bolt.

Thunder crashed outside. Lightning lit the room with flashbulb brilliance. Carl's mind worked the fastest it had in weeks. He could get out now!

He could hot-wire the old man's car and be safe at home by morning. He could leave the old man and his lunatic Heaven far behind.

Wait. No. Not so fast.

He sat by the door for a long time. Listening. Planning. Gathering strength.

From somewhere downstairs he heard the chime of a faraway clock. Midnight.

Alertness splashed over him like a jolt of ice water.

Yes, the old man must be asleep.

And Carl was ready.

He turned the knob. The door opened with a muffled click.

Carl removed his shoes, tucked one into his belt and carried the other: a weapon.

Okay! All set to go!

One deep calming breath and he started down the darkened stairway, advancing slowly, walking on the sides of the steps, back against the wall, trying to minimize the creaking of the ancient boards. There were fifteen steps in all. Carl paused on each one, listening, watching, preparing his balance for the next.

Finally his groping right foot found the soft carpet of the downstairs hall. Home free! He permitted himself a tight smile in the darkness.

The main door, his exit, was at the end of the shadowy thirty-foot hallway. On either side of the door white moonlight shone through narrow panels of cut glass. So close to freedom.

He thought of Lucy. Maybe he could talk some sense into her now. He could tell her about the crazy old man whose religion had made him believe Heaven was on the second floor of his house. What would Lucy say to that? What would the police say?

God, it was almost funny.

Squinting down the dark hall, he was sure one of the doors along either side concealed the sleeping prophet. But which?

It didn't matter.

Now was the time. He'd make a run for it.

Carl began a graceless tiptoed sprint down the carpeted hall. He was pleased with himself for making no noise.

With the exhilaration of a front runner breaking the tape, he reached the door. His prize was waiting for him; he couldn't believe it. The key was in the lock!

He tugged at the door, turning the key at the same time.

Lightning flashed again, throwing the hall into painful light.

But the light didn't go out.

Terror knotted Carl's face. He felt a lump moving in his stomach. Blood seemed to drain from his body, leaving him cold, weak, and afraid as he turned and faced the old man.

The prophet was dressed in a long gray robe. His white hair, wild and abundant, made him look like the mad artist's rendering of a violent Old Testament God.

Carl withered in the old man's stare. From the gnarled hand a revolver's barrel also stared, cold and unblinking.

The old man's voice was like thunder, "You have been a fool, and you've proven yourself a sinner. You have failed your test, revealed the kind of soul you possess. In spite of my warnings, my help, and my prayers, you have yielded to temptation, forever forsaking your place above."

He lifted the revolver with both hands, leveled it at Carl's forehead. "For your transgression, it is the calling of the prophet to see that you are punished. Damnation—that is your fate. Damnation for your sins, now and forever."

And so saying, the old man motioned with his weapon, and pulled open the heavy door to the basement.

❧ Kirby ❧

Kirby was not an imaginary playmate. Lonely as I was in those days, I wasn't the type to make anybody up. At least not anybody like Kirby.

That was back in 1958, when we bought that big old house in Eden Falls, Vermont. The place was way off by itself, some two miles out of town, where it wasn't real easy for me to meet anyone.

We moved there in July, so I had to reconcile myself to a long solitary summer before school would bring me face to face with the other kids from the village. I was ten years old and far too shy to make friends easily.

My mom didn't work outside the house. She stayed home because she had to take care of my little brother, Roddy. He was just a baby, too small to play with, so I hung out by myself most of the time.

Dad was on the road a lot; he traveled around selling all sorts of athletic equipment. And that could keep him away for weeks at a time, driving all over New Hampshire and up into Maine. I liked it when he was around on weekends because he'd play toss with me, or drive us all into town to the Dairy Queen. Sometimes we'd stay to take in a movie at the drive-in. Westerns, usually, because Dad liked them.

When the weekend was over, Dad would leave again. I think my mom got lonely, too. She used to make lots of calls to her sister in Indiana. Then, when Dad got around to paying the bills, they'd fight about the long distance charges, and the grocery expenses and lots of other things. I didn't like to hear them fighting, so even some weekends I'd go off alone. I'd usually stay out in the back of the house where I'd shoot my bow and arrow, or play with my plastic soldiers in the sandy area near the hillside.

I loved that hill behind our house. It began where our lawn ended, then rose steep and rocky and dense with vegetation. Tall trees stretched toward the sky and the sun made fantastic pictures in their leaves. Dark pockets of shadows, deeper than any cave, beckoned, enticing me with almost hypnotic power. That hill offered mystery and the promise of discovery. Nowhere on earth seemed more wild and unexplored.

On top were the railroad tracks, where trains passed twice a day. Sometimes in the morning I'd hear the whistle blowing from miles away. I'd rush outside and wait to hear the cars rumble by, passing invisibly beyond the thickness of trees. When the train passed it shook the earth so much I imagined some wailing monster, like a dinosaur or dragon. And I'd think of myself leading an expedition through that hillside jungle, just like the guy who kidnapped King Kong and carted him away from his island home.

Or at night I'd watch the train's headlight as it passed like a white flying saucer sailing through the treetops. And below, the woods were full of fireflies like a million stars in an endless sky.

At first the woods were off limits to me. Mom was afraid of them. "It's too easy to lose sight of you," she said. But after a while she relented; I was allowed to play among the trees so long as I promised never to go on the tracks. That was fair, I guess, although from time to time I'd sneak to the top of the hill to leave shiny copper pennies on the rails. Then, next day, I'd go back to pick them up, all flattened and funny shaped. Fact is, I didn't have much else to do. As the summer passed, I got quite a collection of flattened copper.

Once when I did that I found not only my penny, but a quarter and a nickel right beside it. They'd squashed out much bigger than my coin. I didn't know who'd left them there and I wasn't sure whether to pick them up.

"Go ahead," a voice said, "I left them for you."

I looked around. There he was, standing behind some blackberry bushes on the other side the track. That's when I saw Kirby for the first time.

I liked him immediately. He grinned a friendly grin that squinched his face up, making him look like a clown without make-up. He seemed about my age, with big bright eyes that sparkled like blue glassies. His spiky red hair was an overgrown crew-cut. "I seen you folks moved into the old Simmons place. Figured it was about time I stop by to say hello. I'm Kirby. What's your name, anyways?"

"Terry," I told him. "You live around here?"

He flipped his arm back, pointing up the tracks with his thumb. "Dad and me got a place up the flats."

"What about your ma?"

"She took off. Dad says she died, but I ain't so sure."

"What d'ya mean?"

"I see her around sometimes. That's all. No big deal. Why don't you pick up your money?"

I took the penny, nickel, and quarter and shoved them down into the pocket of my shorts.

"How come you squashed thirty cents?" I asked. "Jeez, that's enough for three comics, or—"

"I give you thirty cents, you'll spend it, right? I don't want you spendin' somethin' I give you. I want you keepin' it. Besides, I know where there's plenty more. Pirates buried it."

That was my first inkling that Kirby was imaginative. Of course I knew no pirates had buried any stash of modern coins. I bet Kirby knew it, too. But that was the beginning of a fantasy, and, starting right then I think, neither of us wanted to deny a fantasy before we enjoyed it together.

"You wanna see where they hid it?" Kirby asked.

"Okay. Sure."

"Come on."

So began our first adventure, and over the next few months— and the years to come—we'd have plenty more.

During that summer before my first year at Eden Falls Elementary, I spent many afternoons with Kirby. If I had to have only one playmate, I couldn't have blundered on a better one. He was able to abandon himself completely to whatever game we decided to play. Whether it was Roy Rogers or Superman, Flash Gordon or Davy Crockett, Kirby would always give our crude scenarios a quirky depth and immediacy.

I remember once telling him I bet he'd grow up to be a writer because of the neat ideas he came up with. Looking back on it now, they probably weren't so brilliant—in fact, I don't think Kirby was especially smart—but at the time his odd notions had a way of firing my imagination and holding my interest. Certain games, like episodes of a movie serial, would go on for weeks at a time. He created and acted out the part of a mad scientist named Dr. Moon, who invented a silent explosion. And I was hot on the Doctor's trail in the role of Superman.

When we played Flash Gordon the woods between my backyard and the railroad tracks became an alien landscape where brutish creatures toting powerful ray guns lurked and threatened.

Before moving to Eden Falls, I had played similar games with my friend Jimmy Deflippi or with my favorite cousin, Eugene. But things never worked so smoothly: we'd often argue over who was to be the hero, and who was to be the villain. Usually these disputes were settled by angry resignation or reluctant compromise.

But with Kirby there was no need for compromise. He was always delighted to be the bad guy, and that suited me just fine.

Perhaps I didn't realize it at the time, but Kirby's real talent was not in the scenarios he created. His ability lay more in the way he enacted the roles of his villains. A casual observer might conclude that he had tremendous natural acting talent. As mime or mimic, I'd never seen better, even on television. Kirby could imitate anyone from Jerry Lewis to Walt Disney to Marlin Perkins. His face would change, he'd seem fatter or thinner, he'd grow taller, get older. He had an incredible ability to concentrate and project.

But now I think what I witnessed was more than just raw talent.

Kirby was able to abandon himself completely to the part of Dr. Moon, or Montana Jack, or the alien Marzog. Somehow, he was able to actually become those people.

The first time I saw the extent of his talent was when we were playing John Wayne versus the Indian. A brave named Killer Wolf had massacred my family along with a bunch of settlers on the wagon train from Boston. Killer Wolf had then retreated to Haunted Mountain with a coat of bloody scalps. As the lone survivor, it was my duty to go after him and take revenge.

I chased Killer Wolf to a cave hidden among some rocks. As I peered cautiously into the dark opening, Killer Wolf got the drop on me. He circled around from behind, his bow taut, his arrow aimed at my back.

"Turn, White Eyes. See the arrow that will kill you."

Hand on my six-shooter, I slowly about-faced.

Kirby stood beside a horse chestnut tree, his imaginary bow poised before the kill. He had removed his shoes and jersey to play the role of Indian, but, somehow, he had done more than that.

When I looked at him, his white freckled skin actually appeared to be red. A sunburn, I remember thinking.

What's more, his red hair was now black and braided. Slashes of war paint gave demonic emphasis to his cheeks and forehead.

And at that moment I could have sworn his wide blue eyes had turned black as the coal chips along the railroad bed.

Something like very real fear destroyed my John Wayne persona. I couldn't utter a word. I could only stare, open-mouthed.

"I will not kill you now, white man," he said, "because you expect to die. I will kill you when you don't expect. I will kill you when you think you are safe, when you think I have forgotten."

"K... Kirby...," I said, my voice faltering.

He laughed a jolly, friendly laugh and jumped behind a large mossy rock. When he moved into view again, the illusion was gone and he was just Kirby, smiling at me. He dug a packet of baseball cards out of his pocket, ripped off the wrapper and tore the gum in two. He handed me the bigger half and said, "Have some of this jerky; it'll take the hunger pains away."

His voice sounded exactly like John Wayne's.

Sometimes during that first summer Kirby stayed overnight at my house. If it was a warm clear night, Mom would let us sleep in the backyard under a tent we'd made from old blankets and worn-out sheets. We'd lather-up with Old Woodsman's and lie awake, talking and giggling. When morning came we awoke with no recollection of having fallen asleep.

We had good talks on those warm summer nights. We'd look up at the vast black sky where occasional shooting stars crossed the blur of the Milky Way, and we'd speculate about God and the beginning of the universe. Sometimes we'd consider the other civilizations that no doubt lived out there, and what they might be like.

"Boy, I'd really like to see a flying saucer," I said.

"Yeah, me too."

"What would you do if you seen one? Would you run?"

"Na. If they can fly across outer space, they could prob'ly catch me if I run off. I think I'd just stand there and get a good look. I'd really like to see something like that, you know? I bet they're nothin' like we picture 'em."

"But what if they wanted to, you know, take over or something? Like in The War of the Worlds. Aren't you scared they'd blast you like they did that priest and the army guys?"

"Naw."

"How come?"

"'Cause that's what we imagine they'd do. If they really came here, they'd do something we can't even imagine."

"Like what?"

"Like.... How should I know?"

We were quiet for a moment, struggling under the weight of that idea. I bet the picture was the same in both of our minds: our earth, a tiny spinning marble on the endless black parking lot of space.

My Mom liked Kirby a lot, and was happy to have him stay for dinner and the frequent overnights. But he never invited me to go home with him. Sometimes I wondered what his place was like, and I was curious to see his father.

As sleazy as it seems now, what I did seemed perfectly all right at the time. One afternoon I followed Kirby when, as always, he left by walking off down the tracks. I shadowed him until he took a little path that veered off to the right. Leaving plenty of distance between us, I kept him in sight until he walked into his yard.

Immediately, I felt bad about what I had done. I knew then why Kirby never asked me over. He didn't want me to see his house, which was little more than a shack. The roof was made of tarpaper and there was old, broken furniture out front. The yard, closed off with wire fencing, was full of chickens. They roamed and pecked among the junk that littered the unmowed lawn.

There was no car in the yard; maybe they didn't even own one.

The windows were open and not screened. I thought about all the different bugs that could fly into the place.

Soon after Kirby went inside, I got a glimpse of his father through the window. I hung out a while, watching. Although his father never left my sight, I didn't see Kirby again. I wondered if they got along okay.

I wondered what they talked about.

After a while I started feeling guilty about spying, so I ran home and never told anybody what I had done.

Kirby didn't go to Eden Falls Elementary. He told me he went to school in Chester, the next town over. It was weird to think my nearest neighbor lived in a whole different town.

By the time school started we'd become best friends. It was one of those solid, everlasting bonds we all enjoy briefly as children. I wasn't too eager to hang out with the other kids. In fact, they made it easy for me to feel standoffish because no one was especially friendly at first. Mom said I had to be patient and give them time to get used to me.

Like I said, I was pretty shy in those days, so I didn't work too hard to make friends. Besides, I always knew that when I got home at three-thirty Kirby would come sauntering down out of the woods. He'd have a stack of comics with him, or some weird object he'd found, or more likely a terrific new variation on one of our games-in-progress.

Last year had been IGY—International Geophysical Year—so we were always talking about Sputnik and space and all sorts of scientific breakthroughs, real and imagined.

Kirby and I were usually caught up in playing space invasion, patterned after our favorite movie, The War of the Worlds. I was always Dr. Forrester.

Kirby liked to take dramatic, dangerous looking falls, so he'd play victim after victim of the Martian death rays. That is, when he wasn't playing the Martians themselves. We never argued over the role of hero. It was understood. I always got the part.

Not so in real life.

There was this one kid in the sixth grade, Stevie Petty, and he was a bully. Stevie was one of those squatty tree-stump-like kids. He had long, slick-looking hair and always wore this dirty denim jacket. He hung out with some greaser kids from Pikesville who were always shoving kids in the hall, or tripping somebody, or talking dirty and calling people names. Any time you saw him outside school, he'd be spitting after every other word.

Nobody had to tell me it would be a good idea to avoid Stevie and his creepy pals. But avoiding him was one thing, being invisible was another.

"Is your name really Terry?" he asked me in the hall one day.

I nodded cautiously.

"I thought Terry was a girl's name."

Sixth graders had Phys.Ed. right after us. One time when I was still taking my shower, Stevie Petty and his greasy friends slid into the locker room. I was shy about showering, so I'd always sneak in pretty close to last, after most of the other kids had gone back to class.

"Hey, guys, look at this," Stevie said, his barrel-body blocking the door to the shower stall. "Check it out, you guys! One of the girls is still in the shower. Anybody wanna see a naked girl?"

Just then Mr. Stewart the gym teacher came in, so I took off quick.

A couple days later I stayed in town after school. Kirby and I were going for Cokes at the drugstore where we could check out what was new in comic books and monster magazines.

It was a quick walk from the school to the drugstore if you cut through Proctor's backyard, then took the alley that connected Pleasant Street with Main Street.

I was walking through that alley when I saw Stevie and his hoody friends out behind Cobb's IGA. They were sitting on milk cartons and smoking cigarettes.

I saw them almost in time to turn back.

"Hey Terry-girl, come on over and show us yer pussy," Stevie said before spitting on the ground.

"Di'n't you see enough of it in the shower the other day?" some guy answered back.

I turned around and started to vacate when this guy called Fark—short for Farquhar, I think—pulled up on his bike. He was another one of Stevie's scummy cronies and he cut short my retreat.

Half a dozen of them quickly formed a ring around me and Stevie. Of course, I had a pretty good idea what was coming. Heroes like John Wayne and Flash Gordon and Dr. Forrester seemed a thousand miles away. And Superman had never seemed more like a fantasy.

I looked at that line of leering faces forming a corral around me and planned to run away just as quick as I decided which two kids formed the weakest link in the human chain. Stevie shoved me in the shoulder. I staggered backward, then somebody pushed me back toward Stevie.

"Some people say it ain't nice to pick on girls," Stevie said as he put his flat hand against my breast and squeezed. "All you gotta do is say, 'It ain't nice to pick on girls,' an' I'll leave you alone. See? Easy as pie...."

He spat on the ground right beside my sneaker. Then he pinched my nipple. Hard. It would be black and blue for a week.

"Jes' say it, Terry-girl, and I'll let you off this time." I noticed his knuckles were dirty as he balled his fingers into a fist.

Cobb's IGA and Noel's Five-and-Dime were separated by another alley, a walkway, really, less than three feet wide. Just when I thought I was going to get creamed, somebody called from that narrow alleyway, "Stephen, Stephen! Does your mother really do it with cripples?"

I had no idea what the voice was talking about, but whatever it was sure struck a nerve in Stevie. "Sonavabitch," he said and he burst from the circle, shouldering two of his stupid friends out of the way. He tore like an angry bull toward the narrow alley.

Before I knew what was happening, he disappeared inside.

Almost immediately I heard the most soul-shattering cry of terror I've ever heard in my life.

Stevie Petty came staggering backward from the alley. When he was clear of the opening, he turned. His face was white as chalk dust, his eyes wide and glazed. His mouth hung open; the muscles in his cheeks looked like they were paralyzed.

Then he started to run, his chunky arms and legs pumping like crazy. I can't recall ever seeing a human being move so fast. When the guys surrounding me saw their leader beating a retreat in obvious terror, they moved after him, bumping into each other and crying out as if the horror were contagious.

My eyes were glued on the mouth of the alley, and I started backing away, not sure if I dared turn my back on it long enough to run.

In a moment Kirby walked out of the alley. His happy face was wrinkled in a bright smile and he was laughing with obvious delight. "Thought I was su'pose to meet you at the soda fountain," he said. Then he giggled like he'd just heard the funniest joke in the world.

Over Cherry Cokes, and during the rest of the school year, I tried to get Kirby to tell me what he had done to Stevie Petty in that alleyway. All he'd ever say was, "I never touched him. I just showed him how much of a retard he is."

But I'll never forget that look on Stevie Petty's face. It was as if he'd got a close-up look at the devil.

During the next week, however, maybe I got a hint of what had happened.

Somehow Kirby and I got it into our heads that millions of years ago pilgrims from outer space had colonized earth in much the same way as European pilgrims colonized the new world.

Of course this notion provoked tough theological questions about creation and evolution, but we didn't get too bogged down with them. Still, in one of our front porch philosophical sessions, we tried on the idea that maybe creation had occurred on one of the other planets, and certain of the creations had evolved into human beings who had relocated here.

This slightly forbidden thinking resulted in a favorite new game that took place millions of years ago when only spacemen lived on earth. In the woods behind my house those spacemen were apt to encounter creatures far more frightening than prehistoric lizards. Very likely some of those creatures might be intelligent. Vastly intelligent. And armed.

I was Davy Rocket, the space age counterpart of our favorite frontiersman. The railroad track was a hilltop landing platform for interplanetary vehicles; the wilderness around it was an unexplored jungle where unknown terrors might be lurking.

As the game started, my sidekick Mike (who never had a last name and was always played by Kirby) and I had discovered a crashed ship that seemed to be of alien origin.

"Careful. They might have some kind of power we don't even know about," Mike cautioned.

"Yeah," I said. "Better keep your rayblaster fully charged."

"Yes, sir."

This was not to be a good day for Mike. We hadn't traveled far along the alien's trail when a gun battle ensued. Whizzing rays split the air. Trees and rocks changed color before vanishing in a bright pulse of light. Our rocket was destroyed and Mike took a blast to the face.

Lying on the stony ground, Mike took his last feeble breath.

"You're the best friend I ever had," he told me. Then he died, leaving me alone to track the killcrazy spaceman.

At this point Kirby switched roles. With Mike's body safely buried, he became the alien. I gave him a few minutes to run ahead and hide while I said some words above the grave of my fallen comrade. With my rayblaster ready and vengeance in my heart, I set off to find the savage friend-killer.

It was twilight in the woods. Dark shale outcroppings looked like crouching beasts. Trees reached forward with gnarled limbs, witches' hands, groping for my throat. Pools of shadows appeared like sinister caverns in the landscape.

It was often my habit to give voice-over narration, outlining the story's action as the suspense built. "Davy Rocket arrives in a place that looks like a campsite. He looks around. Yes, the spaceman must have been here, and not too long ago. Davy knows he has to be careful and keep still, or he'll give himself away. If the spaceman gets a shot at him, it will mean the death of earth," or something like that.

The truth is, a fair amount of real suspense built up. Kirby was always unpredictable and he had a tricky imagination. I suspected he might have some real surprises in store for me, so I was ever on my guard. I held my breath; my heart pounded like a tom-tom. As I squinted into the darkening woodland, I was afraid to break concentration even long enough to blink.

Standing very still, biting my lower lip, I heard a twig snap. Then the swishing rustle of fallen leaves, as if a big lizard was slithering through the woods toward me.

"Davy Rocket has no idea what the spaceman looks like. He could be a giant, he could be some kinda blobby thing with a hundred mouths, he could be—"

And then I saw the spaceman.

It was Kirby, I knew, but when he stepped out from behind that thick-trunked maple, it wasn't Kirby I saw.

Perhaps it was the work of our youthful imaginations, perhaps it was the peculiar play of the fading sun as it filtered through the rich green leaves, perhaps it was an incredible fantasy of light and shadow as they painted themselves across Kirby's skin. I don't know what it was, but to this day I remember the illusion as if it had happened just moments ago.

The thing standing above me on the slope seemed to be an elongated man. He must have stood seven, maybe eight feet tall. His skin was green as a grass snake's and his eyes glowed a fiery yellow, like the very tip of a flame. His jaw protruded into a muzzle. It worked

up and down alligator style, showing two rows of fanglike teeth.
He aimed something at me. It must have been a stick, but it
looked like some crazy kind of space age weapon.

By now, of course, I was somewhat used to Kirby's imitations
and transformations, but there was something about this one that
burned me with terror. I threw down my plastic space gun and
backed up, preparing to run away.

The pitch of the hill caused me to fall. I tumbled down a good
ten feet before realizing Kirby was running after me, shouting.

"Terry, wait! Come back!"

I risked a glance over my shoulder and saw Kirby tearing after
me. His face showed a mixture of fright and sorrow.

"Wait, Terry!"

And he looked just the way he should, his crew-cut a rusty
crown on his head, his t-shirt flapping like loose skin, his blue den-
ims soiled at the knees with grass stains and mud.

I ran and ran and when I stopped, leaning against the back door
to our garage, Kirby was right behind me.

I guess I felt safe with the solid bulk of my house at my back. I
tried to smile at Kirby, but I was breathing too rapidly and my heart
was pounding at a disturbing rate.

"I... I'm sorry, Terry," he said. "I'm awful sorry."

By the time we were seniors, I had my driver's license. A part-
time job at Whitcome's Grain Store earned me money enough to
buy a Chevy junker to fix up. It was good enough to get me around,
but the best thing was not having to take the bus back and forth to
the union school in Chester.

I didn't see Kirby too much anymore. We should have been
classmates, but he'd dropped out and took a job as a short order
cook at a diner in Bellows Falls. At least that's what he told me.

The year before, I had met Launa Clemens in my algebra class.
We started spending a lot of time together during school and after,
but Kirby was never interested in tagging along. From my point of
view it was just as well. He was still my friend, sure, but Launa was...
well, she was something new and very special.

She was blonde and pretty and soft-spoken, with a frail physique and a non-aggressive manner. And she had an attentive
way about her that always made me feel important, as if I were

the classiest guy in the world.

I can't remember specifically how we passed all our time together; I just remember how fast it went. We'd drive to the shopping plaza in Springfield for sodas and hamburgers. We'd take in movies or, during the summer, we'd spend whole days at the lake. The hours passed blissfully. Life seemed simple and good. I had little inclination to do much of anything if it was not with Launa. She was in my thoughts all the time. Her face seemed to hover between my eyes and my homework. I'd stare blankly out the window with her soft words whispering in my memory. Every night I fell asleep with Launa on my mind.

Very quickly we started talking about going to the same college. Sometimes we discussed skipping college altogether to get married and start a family. Even now I recall our time together as something more than simple infatuation. I know most relationships might be dismissed as puppy love at that age, but I believe two people can occasionally find something elegant and right; it's perfect from the start and it never changes. It was that way with us, I think, but we never had an opportunity to find out.

She died.

She didn't suffer, her mother told me. She died quietly in bed one night with my senior picture on the pillow beside her.

Perhaps it isn't right for one so young to experience death, or such a great sorrow. I surely had nothing in my life to prepare me for such a blow. For a while I tried to be angry with Launa because she'd never told me that her quiet ways and frail physique were the result of a weak heart.

But I couldn't be angry.

My appetite vanished and I lost weight. I withdrew from my family, spending long hours alone in my room. My studies suffered. Though I didn't fail any subjects, I skipped my graduation ceremonies.

Mom and Dad wanted me to see a doctor. When the appointments came, I'd drive off in my car but could never bring myself to go to the clinic and talk to him.

A couple of times Kirby came by the house. He'd try to cheer me up with funny stories or his silly imitations of certain characters around town. I had always laughed at the way he did Mr. Cobb, the absent-minded grocer, and his tough-guy imitation of Stevie Petty was always hilarious. Kirby called him T.V. Spitty.

But my laughter didn't come easily anymore.

"I wish I could make you feel better," Kirby said. "I wish there was something I could do. You're my friend, my only friend. I'd do anything for you."

I was touched, but I couldn't reply. On some level I knew that if I didn't snap out of it, in time even Kirby would give up on me. But I couldn't. I just couldn't.

One day when Dad was out selling and Mom and Roddy were in Springfield shopping, Kirby stopped by the house. I was sitting on the porch smoking a cigarette. Mom had left me a glass of lemonade on the railing, but I hadn't touched it.

"Hi, Terr," Kirby said. He had changed quite a bit since I'd first met him eight years ago. He'd matured with a rough and robust rotundity that made him look powerful but, frankly, unattractive. Maybe that's why he'd never taken up with a girlfriend. As a minor concession to style, he wore his red hair longer now, but his freckled face was blotchy with acne.

"What'd you do," I asked, "take the day off?"

"Naw, I quit. Cooking with all that grease ain't no good for the complexion." He laughed.

I smiled without enthusiasm. "Got something else lined up?"

"Nope. Think I'm gonna travel. Hitch around the country or somethin'."

That stung me. I hadn't been seeking Kirby's company lately, but the idea of not having him around was oddly painful. He'd been part of my life now for a lot of years. He was my only real friend and I didn't fancy the idea of losing him.

"You serious?"

"Yup. Nothing much happening to keep me here."

"What about your dad?"

"What about him? Think he gives a shit what I do?"

"You sure about this, Kirb?"

"Yup. Mostly. But I want to talk about it some. That's why I come by. Wanna go for a drive?"

"Sure, I guess."

"We'll stop at Mr. Cobb's for a six-pack. I got the old boy

convinced I'm eighteen years old."

I drove us up to the quarry off Lover's Lane Road. It was a popular spot, but not during the daytime. That afternoon Kirby and I were the only ones there.

When we were in junior high we used to come here a lot on our bicycles. We'd stretch out on flat rocks and study the three seventy-foot cliffs that surrounded the little square of water. In those days we used to go swimming in our underwear.

The rock had warmed in the sunshine. Kirby took off his jersey and rolled it up into a pillow.

"Where you plannin' to go?" I asked, the cold bottom of the beer can made a wet circle on my t-shirt.

"Dunno. Away. Thought you might like to come, too. You got a car. I could buy the gas. We'd be partners like them guys on Route 66."

I closed my eyes. With the sun on my eyelids, everything looked red. In silence, I thought about leaving Eden Falls.

"I don't know what I want to do," I told him. "I got accepted at Middlebury and Cornell."

"So you goin' to college, or what?"

I shook my head lazily, not knowing, and took a pull of beer.

Kirby crushed his can and tossed it out into the water.

"Terry, you gotta do somethin'. Launa took a chunk outa your life, sure, but you gotta find somethin' to fill it up with."

I looked at him. His eyes were glassy. I couldn't say anything. After a while I said, "I don't know, Kirby."

We finished the six-pack pretty much in silence. I wasn't used to drinking, and three cans had me spinning a little. I started to cry.

Kirby stood up, looking uncomfortable. "I gotta take a piss," he said and wandered off. I could hear him rustling through the bushes somewhere in the distance.

The sun warmed my face and the warm stone felt pleasant on my back. The beer relaxed me, tugging my mind toward sleep.

Maybe I dreamed. Maybe I awoke with someone's hand on my chest. Fingers scratched the skin under my t-shirt. Something brushed my lips, then flexed against them with a slow moist suction.

It was a dream, I think.

When I opened my eyes Launa was kneeling beside me. Her

shirt was off and her small perfect breasts were white as paper in the afternoon sun. As she lowered her head, her long blonde hair fell on either side of my face, forming a private silken tent in which our lips did their secret business.

It felt like a dream with her doe-soft eyes peering eagerly at me every time I opened mine.

I wrapped my arms around her and felt embarrassed as I started growing hard.

Then I knew.

I pushed her away and she rolled off the rock.

I stood up spitting, wiping my mouth with the side of my hand. Fully awake now, anger flared like an explosion of gasoline.

It was Kirby on his hands and knees, looking up at me.

"But Terry, I wanted—"

I kicked him in the gut and jumped on his stomach when he toppled. The breath shot out of him like beer-scented wind.

I snatched up a rock and pounded him with it. It tore along the side of his forehead, stripping hair from his temple.

And when I realized what I was doing, I stopped. I crawled off him and got to my feet, then bolted toward my car.

Thoughts racing, eyes blurred with tears, I sped along the roads, not knowing where I was going. Not caring. "I'm sorry, I'm sorry," I screamed over and over, but I'm not sure who I was talking to.

I never saw Kirby again.

I'm not sure if I killed him. Sometimes I think I did. But when I calmed down and drove back to the quarry to find him, he wasn't there.

Maybe he found his way home. But I don't think so. Some days later I went back to the place where he lived with his father. No one was there. The shack was deserted and thoroughly vandalized. It was as if it had been empty for a long time.

Maybe he ran off, began his hitchhiking tour of the country. Maybe he's still on the road. I hope he's found some place to settle down.

But sometimes, when I look up at the black and endless sky, I think of that unnamable thing about Kirby, that thing that was special, that talent I'd witnessed but never understood. He could be there now, a star in the sky, a tree in the forest, a snake basking on some sun-warmed stone wall. He's somewhere, I hope.

I hope Kirby found his place.

And if he was not lucky enough to find anyone like himself, I pray he found someone to be like.

I'm sorry it wasn't me. But I miss him.

❧ Swan Song? ❧

*M*y final piece of short fiction was published in the December 18-25, 2002 issue of Seven Days, *Burlington's weekly news and arts newspaper. The editors had invited seven local writers to speculate on the fate of an abandoned building on Shelburne Road: The Panda Inn. This once popular Chinese restaurant had been vacant since 1999 when two co-owners were murdered there. After the police investigation, the place was sealed. Everything remained exactly as it was the night of the murders. It was a time capsule.*

Needless to say, The Panda Inn soon acquired a sinister air.

In addition to being the last short story I ever wrote, this is also the shortest, a mere 410 words.

Seven Days *supplied the seven writers with the first sentence; we had to take it from there . . .*

❧ The Last Fortune Cookie ❧

For three years the tables at the Panda had been sitting undisturbed, the soy sauce and chopsticks collecting dust. But all that's about to change. A little fancy picking, and I'm inside. Quick look around. Interior's weird, frozen in time, like those old atom-bomb movies—everything's ready for business, but no customers come.

The kitchen. Dishes stacked neat. Dishwasher open and full. String beans in a colander look like brown twisted roots. Body outlines, two of them, chalked on the floor tiles.

This is going to be easy: in and out in 15 minutes. By daybreak, it's roast Panda. By breakfast, I'm paid and gone while my employer waits for his insurance check.

Makes sense. Place won't sell, just sucks up taxes. Couple deaths like that, people figure it's haunted, maybe cursed. Christ, they couldn't even hire a cleaning crew.

Let's see... Fire's gotta start in the kitchen.

Frickin' odd! Must be the light or something. That body outline—the one on the left—I thought both arms were at its side. Now one's out-stretched, pointing, like it's moved.

Jesus! Something stinks. I turn around. Bloated blue fish are decomposing in the feng shui aquarium, floating in a foul-smelling soup.

Makes me wanna hurl, but there's work to do.

I haul my tool kit, a big plastic garbage bag, into the kitchen. I extract the putrid sleeping bag I swiped from some bum and smooth it out nice and cozy in the corner by the sink. Add a couple empty booze bottles, a few handfuls of trash from McDonald's, and a bunch of crumpled cigarette packs. Voila! A bum's nest! Looks like he's been camping here a while. Should've been more careful with his cigarettes. . .

I light one up. Sprinkle alcohol on the bedbag. A few puffs, a quick flick, and I'll do a little Chinese cooking of my own.

What the hell? Must've been seeing double. Now there's only one outline on the floor.

"And that's how you found him?"

"Yes sir, just like that. Sitting there at the table."

"Looks like a squatter, Lieutenant. There's a bedroll in the kitchen."

"Too well-dressed for a squatter. Funny thing is the food."

"Funny?"

"Yeah. He's sitting there dead and, look, it's like somebody served him a meal. He's got wonton soup and a plate of General Tsao's Chicken in front of him. It's all fresh. When I got here the rice was still steaming."

❧ NOTES ❧

"Them Bald-headed Snays" was written for and appeared in *Masques III*, edited by J.N. Williamson and published by St. Martin's Press in 1989.

"Soul Keeper" was written for and appeared in *Lovecraft's Legacy*, edited by Robert E. Weinberg and Martin H. Greenberg, published by Tor Books in 1990.

"Penetration" was written for and appeared in *Thunder's Shadow*, edited by Erik Secker, Winfield, Illinois, 1994.

"Kirby" was written for and appeared in *After The Darkness*, edited by Stanley Wiater, published by Maclay & Associates in 1993.

"The Last Fortune Cookie" was written for and appeared in *Seven Days*, a news and arts weekly, published in Burlington, Vermont. December 18-25, 2002.

ꝯ About the Author ꝯ

Joseph A. Citro (on right) is an expert in New England weirdness. In over a dozen publications—novels and nonfiction—he has guided readers through a dark, disturbing, and often sinister landscape traditionally portrayed with sunny skies above quaint villages. His nonfiction books include *Passing Strange, Cursed in New England*, and many more. Additionally, Mr. Citro has authored five acclaimed novels, among them *Shadow Child, Lake Monsters*, and *Deus-X: The Reality Conspiracy*.

Not Yet Dead is his only collection of short fiction. Of the stories included here, one ("Snays") was chosen for *The Year's Best Fantasy and Horror* and had been reprinted in several other anthologies. "Soul Keeper" was turned unto a motion picture. Other work has been adapted for radio, stage, and TV. You can reach him on Facebook or via the electronic Ouija board at . . .

BLOG: http://josephacitro.blogspot.com
WEB: http://www.josephacitro.com

Curious about other Crossroad Press books?
Stop by our site:
http://store.crossroadpress.com
We offer quality writing
in digital, audio, and print formats.

Enter the code FIRSTBOOK
to get 20% off your first order from our store!
Stop by today!

CPSIA information can be obtained at www.ICGtesting.com
Printed in the USA
BVOW03s2135110813

327869BV00005B/59/P